www.KendallvilleLibrary.org   2009-06
260-343-2010   KDLVL-LIM

Let's go hiking

ADVENTURES OUTDOORS™

Let's Go
HIKING

Suzanne Slade

PowerKiDS press™

New York

With much love to my orienteering, rock-climbing, New Zealand-tramping, Mt. Rainier-climbing, Appalachian Trail-hiking buddy—my husband, Mike.

Published in 2007 by The Rosen Publishing Group, Inc.
29 East 21st Street, New York, NY 10010

First Edition

Editor: Amelie von Zumbusch
Book Design: Dean Galiano and Erica Clendening
Layout Design: Julio Gil

Photo Credits: Cover, p. 4 © www.istockphoto.com/Ulrike Hammerich; p. 5 © www.istockphoto.com/Midwest Wilderness; pp. 6, 7, 8, 12, 14, 17, 18, 20, 21, 22, 26, 28 © www.shutterstock.com; p. 10 © www.istockphoto.com/Muriel Lasure; p. 11 © www.istockphoto.com/Alan Heartfield; p. 16 Courtesy of Suzanne Slade; p. 19 © www.istockphoto.com/William Walsh; p. 24 © www.istockphoto.com/Bill Koplitz; p. 25 © www.istockphoto.com/Paige Falk; p. 27 © www.istockphoto.com/Jim Jurica.

Library of Congress Cataloging-in-Publication Data

Slade, Suzanne.
    Let's go hiking / Suzanne Slade. — 1st ed.
       p. cm. — (Adventures outdoors)
    Includes index.
    ISBN-13: 978-1-4042-3651-6 (library binding)
    ISBN-10: 1-4042-3651-1 (library binding)
    1. Hiking—Juvenile literature.   I. Title.
  GV199.52.S53 2007
  796.51—dc22
                                                    2006021037

Manufactured in the United States of America

Contents

Hiking

Hiking is going on a walk to explore your surroundings. You can hike across a flat meadow, through shaded woods, or up a steep mountain. You can even hike across a noisy city. A hiking trip may last for an hour or a couple of weeks. Hikers have

This family is hiking in Alberta's Banff National Park. National parks offer many beautiful hiking trails.

Many people like hiking with dogs, but some parks do not allow pets. Check the rules before bringing your dog.

the freedom to choose the type of hiking trip that is right for them.

People enjoy hiking because they often discover new things. Hikers also like to learn about nature. Many people hike because it helps them relax. Hiking is a great way to get exercise as you enjoy fresh air and the company of good friends.

Preparing for Your Hiking Trip

Before leaving for your hiking trip, you should spend time choosing a trail that is right for you. Some people like trails that are flat and smooth. Other hikers want a more challenging route. They prefer hiking over hills or across rocky **terrain**. It is important to consider everyone in your hiking group when you select an area in which to go hiking.

Steep mountain trails are challenging to hike, but they often offer striking sights, such as waterfalls.

These trail blazes, or signs, tell you that the red trail goes straight ahead and the orange trail turns left.

Most state parks have hiking trails. State parks usually supply maps that show the length and **difficulty** of each trail. Park trails often have signs that help keep you from getting lost. Some trails will lead you to beautiful sights, such as rivers and waterfalls.

Hiking Gear

Your most important piece of hiking gear is a good pair of shoes or boots. Boots provide support and protection for your feet. Make sure to choose a pair that is not too heavy. Shoes with good **traction** and thick soles work well, too. Buy shoes with cloth on top. Cloth keeps shoes light and allows sweat to escape. Make sure your boots or shoes are not too big or small. Footwear that does not fit properly will make your feet hurt and could cause a **blister**.

Wear layers of thin clothing when you go hiking. If you get hot or cold, you can remove or add a layer to stay comfortable. If the weather report indicates the possibility of rain, take a raincoat along.

Some hikers use hiking poles to help them balance when they are walking over rough ground.

Hitting the Trail

Now that you have the proper gear, you are ready to hit the trail. Beginning hikers should choose marked trails. Marked trails have signs along the way so you will not get lost. Most parks provide maps of their marked trails. On the map you will see the length and difficulty of each trail. Trails are labeled easy, moderate, hard, or very hard. Easy

It is a good idea to consult the map in a park before heading off on your hike.

Many trails cross streams or rivers. Some trails have bridges, but others use stepping-stones or fallen logs.

trails are generally short. They will take you over flat land or small hills. Hard trails are longer and include rough, steep areas. If you are new to hiking, start with an easy trail and work up to more difficult trails.

There are three types of trails. They are in-and-out, point-to-point, and loop. On an in-and-out trail, you hike to the end of the trail and then walk

back to the beginning. A point-to-point trail begins in one place and ends at another. When hiking a point-to-point trail, you will need someone to pick you up at the end. A loop trail goes around a path shaped like a circle. You will end up back where you started on a loop trail.

No matter what type of trails you hike, they all begin at a place called the trailhead. As you set off hiking from a trailhead, you never know what adventures you will find on the trail ahead.

DID YOU KNOW?

The first Saturday in June is National Trails Day. People celebrate hiking on this day. Many people pick up litter from trails. Some parks offer special classes on hiking and hiking gear.

This girl is hiking on a trail in the Rocky Mountains in Colorado.

Day Hikes

Many people enjoy going hiking for a day. Day hiking does not require a lot of extra gear. When choosing a trail for a day hike, you need to make sure you have enough hours of sunlight in which to complete it. It is a good idea to tell others about your hiking route and when you plan to return.

If you are going to hike for more than a few hours, you might bring a small backpack along. Depending on the length of your hike, you may need sunblock, a first aid kit, bug spray, food, and drinks. Do not forget your camera! You can take pictures of your hiking buddies and the beautiful sights along the trail.

Take water with you on a hike. Take along extra water if you are hiking on a hot summer day.

Overnight Hikes

Some hikers like to spend several days exploring trails. They enjoy sleeping under the stars at night. Overnight hikes give you time to relax and discover new things in nature.

Hiking overnight is called backpacking. Backpackers take gear for sleeping and cooking. In addition to the usual hiking supplies, they bring a

These people are backpacking in New Zealand. New Zealand has many beautiful places to hike.

These backpackers have set up camp on the side of a mountain.

tent, sleeping bag, flashlight, matches, food, and water. Most people also bring wood or a small stove with which to cook food. When hiking overnight, plan ahead so you will know where you can set up a tent.

Hiking requires a great deal of energy. You should eat often when you hike for several days. A bag of your favorite snack, such as nuts or raisins, will help you keep on hiking!

Hiking in All Kinds of Weather

Hiking is a sport you can do in all seasons and in any weather. Many people like to hike in the autumn so they can see the colorful fall **foliage**. Winter snow and ice change trails into beautiful white wonderlands. Hikers in the spring and summer enjoy warm weather and lots of wildlife.

Make sure to wear plenty of layers of clothing when you go hiking in the winter.

If you go hiking in the spring or summer, you can see lots of rare and beautiful wildflowers.

No matter what time of year you go hiking, always check the weather report before you leave home. Be sure to wear a hat, gloves, and clothes that will keep you warm on cold days. Bring a raincoat if there is a chance of rain. Wear **waterproof** footwear when hiking in the rain or snow.

Orienteering

Orienteering is using a map and a **compass** to figure out your location. Many hikers use orienteering skills to know where they are during a hike. An orienteer uses a special map called a **topographic map**. A topographic map shows the height of certain land features, such as hills, mountains, and valleys. A compass always points north and tells hikers in which direction they are traveling.

Some orienteers enjoy competing in orienteering contests. At these events people race across a large

A topographic map's brown lines show how high the land is. The blue areas on the map are water.

Knowing how to read a map is one of the most important skills a hiker can have.

course. Using only a map and compass for guidance, they must find different spots called controls on the course. The racers must visit each control in a certain order. An orienteer needs to choose the best route and be in good shape to win.

Mountaineering

Hikers who enjoy high adventure and new challenges often learn how to go **mountaineering**. Mountaineers climb steep mountains for fun. They learn special skills that allow them to climb over rocks and ice.

When climbing up a steep area, mountaineers hold ropes fastened to the ground for safety. On rocky terrain climbers wear a harness, which is tied to a rope. They use special tools, such as an ice hammer and crampons, for climbing through snow and ice. Crampons are metal devices that fasten to the bottom of boots. They have sharp metal points, which help a climber dig into snow and ice. After a difficult climb, mountaineers are rewarded with breathtaking views from the top of a mountain.

This mountaineer is climbing an iceberg. Icebergs are huge pieces of ice that broke off from an ice sheet.

Popular Hiking Trails

One of the most popular hiking trails in the United States is the Appalachian Trail. The Appalachian Trail is 2,175 miles (3,500 km) long. It stretches from Georgia to Maine and crosses through 14 different states. People can hike the Appalachian Trail on a short day trip or continue hiking on it for many days and hundreds of miles (km). It cuts through eight national forests and is home to thousands of wild animals.

The northern end of the Appalachian Trail is Maine's Mount Katahdin, seen here.

California's 212-mile- (341 km) long John Muir Trail is the longest stretch of wilderness on the PCT.

On the West Coast, people enjoy hiking the Pacific Crest Trail (PCT). This 2,500-mile (4,023 km) trail goes from Canada to Mexico. The PCT offers various hiking terrains, such as deserts, mountains, volcanoes, and rain forests. Favorite stops on this trail include Yosemite National Forest, Mount Rainier, and the Mojave Desert.

DID YOU KNOW?
It takes about five million steps to walk the Appalachian Trail. Only 8,000 people have hiked the entire trail.

Hiking and Nature

Observing wild animals in nature is one of the most exciting parts of hiking. You can watch for birds perched in trees, deer running through woods, or chipmunks hiding under leaves. It is fun to find animals, but remember to stay a safe distance from them.

Hikers take care of nature. They do not leave trash or food on a trail. If you spot some litter while hiking, pick it up. You can leave the trail cleaner than

Bison are North America's biggest land animal. You can see bison at Yellowstone National Park.

Trout lilies are wildflowers that grow in the United States and Canada. They can be white or yellow.

DID YOU KNOW?

Some plants, such as poison oak and poison ivy, can make your skin break out in a rash, or hives. Protect yourself by wearing long socks and pants. Before you go hiking, check out a book from the library that will help you identify poisonous plants.

you found it. Make sure you do not pollute the water near trails with soap or human waste. You can enjoy looking at the plants and flowers on a trail without picking them. Hikers keep trails beautiful for the next visitor.

Let's Go Hiking!

With a pair of sturdy, comfortable shoes, you can hike anywhere in the world. You might go hiking with one friend or with a large group of people. Hiking is a great way to visit new places and try new things.

On a snowy day, you could try hiking with snowshoes. Snowshoes are large, flat paddles that fasten to the bottom of your shoes. Some people enjoy going on a night hike. They like to find animals that come out after dark. You might see bats swooping through the night sky or hear a hooting owl. Put on a **headlamp** to help you spot other small creatures on the trail. Hiking trails are full of wildlife and exciting adventures. What are you waiting for? Let's go hiking!

Snowshoes let you walk on top of the snow when it is too deep to walk through.

Safety Tips

- Carry a first aid kit when you go out hiking.

- Always hike with at least one other person.

- Pay attention to the trail as you walk. There may be large rocks, tree roots, or sticks you could trip over.

- Pack plenty of water for your hike. Take frequent breaks to rest and drink. When you exercise or the weather is warm, your body needs extra water.

- Do not try to hike too far in one day. Just go as far as you feel comfortable going.

- Take extra care when hiking on rocks. Go slowly so you do not twist an ankle.

- Always let someone know where you are going to hike and when you plan to return.

- You may find some tempting berries on a hike, but don't eat them. Some plants and berries are poisonous.

- If you find animals, such as bears or snakes, do not approach them. Remain calm and back away from them slowly.

- If you lose your fellow hikers, stay where you are and call out for them. If you continue hiking, they will have trouble finding you.

Glossary

blister (BLIS-tur) A sore place that looks like a bubble on the skin, often caused by a bug bite or a burn.

compass (KUM-pus) A tool made up of a freely turning magnetic needle that tells which direction is north.

difficulty (DIH-fih-kul-tee) How hard something is to do or understand.

foliage (FOH-lee-ij) Leaves, flowers, or branches of plants.

headlamp (HED-lamp) A light that is worn on the forehead.

mountaineering (MOWN-tuh-nir-ing) The sport of climbing steep mountains.

orienteering (or-ee-un-TIR-ing) The sport of using a map and a compass to find your way around.

terrain (tuh-RAYN) A piece of land or the qualities of a piece of land.

topographic map (tah-puh-GRA-fik MAP) A type of map that shows different regions, such as mountains, lakes, and forests.

traction (TRAK-shun) The grip a moving object has on a surface.

waterproof (WAH-ter-proof) Not able to get wet.

Index

Web Sites

Due to the changing nature of Internet links, PowerKids Press has developed an online list of Web sites related to this book. This site is updated regularly. Please use this link to access the list: www.powerkidslinks.com/adout/hiking/